My Dad Is Always Working
First Published in 2022 by
THE ISLAMIC FOUNDATION

Distributed by
KUBE PUBLISHING LTD
Tel +44 (0)1530 249230
E-mail: info@kubepublishing.com
Website: www.kubepublishing.com

Author Hafsah Dabiri
Illustrator Arwa Salameh

A Cataloguing-in-Publication Data record for this
book is available from the British Library

ISBN 978-0-86037-841-9
eISBN 978-0-86037-846-4

Printed in China

My Dad
Is Always
WORKING

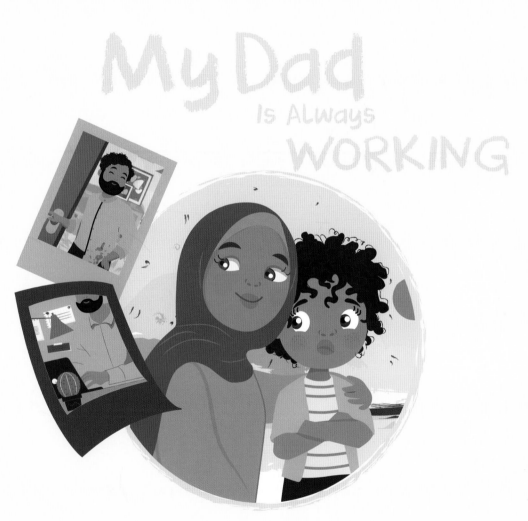

Author: Hafsah Dabiri

Illustrator: Arwa Salameh

"Wake up Abdullah,"
Mum said, "it's time for class."

Abdullah moaned and peeked his head out
from under his duvet.

"Already?" Abdullah complained as he rolled
out of bed and gave his mum a hug. His
clothes were laid out at the end of his bed,
ready for him to take a shower and put on.

As he rushed downstairs for breakfast, his dad whizzed past him with some black smudges on his shirt, looking extremely tired.

Abdullah knew that when his dad was rushing around that fast, on a Sunday morning, he was going to work and he was late!

Abdullah sighed and shouted, "As salaam alaikum Daddy," as his dad opened the door to leave the house.

"Walaikum as salaam," Dad called back out of breath, "I'll come and pick you up from your classes today, insha Allah."

4

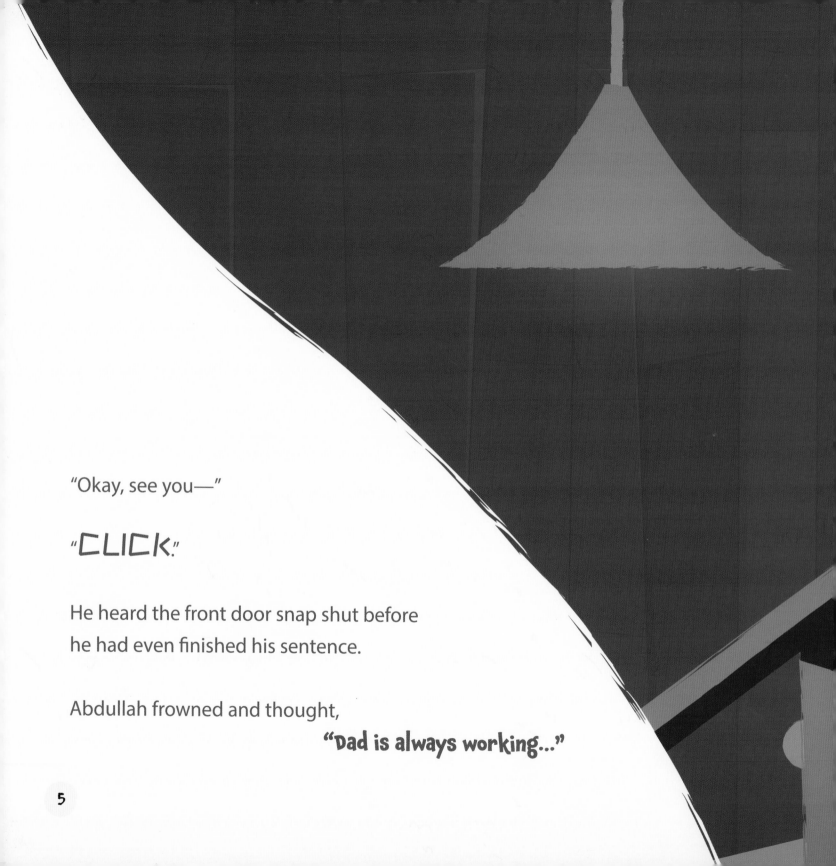

"Okay, see you—"

"CLICK."

He heard the front door snap shut before
he had even finished his sentence.

Abdullah frowned and thought,

"Dad is always working..."

He made his way to the kitchen to have breakfast.

His mum had made him his favourite chocolate and strawberry pancakes for breakfast. A small smile appeared on Abdullah's face and he quickly stuffed his mouth with the delicious, warm, fluffy goodness.

Mum saw that Abdullah was feeling a bit down. "You can ride your bike to class with Khalid today, if you'd like," she suggested.

Abdullah's smile widened, just as his mum thought it would, and he ran out of the house and grabbed his bike.

He was pulling the door closed when he heard his mum shout, "Don't forget your football boots for break time, Abdullah."

"As salaam alaikum children," said Mualimah Lateefah, "we have a fun lesson planned for today! Let's talk about saying thank you."

The students smiled excitedly as they all sat down ready for the class to begin.

"Does anyone know how we thank people in Islam?" asked Mualimah Lateefah.

"I do," said Maryam, "we say JazakAllah Khair."

"Yes, that's right! Well done Maryam," Mualimah Lateefah smiled, "and this means, may God reward you with goodness."

At the end of class she said, "Today, instead of doing some writing for homework, I want you to make your very own cards. So, think about it carefully and make a 'JazakAllah Khair' card for the person who you think deserves your thanks and gratitude."

Maryam turned with a smile and whispered to Abdullah, "I am going to make a card for my mum, of course."

At home time, Abdullah stood in the playground waiting eagerly for his dad to get there so he could talk to him about the project.

"Abdullah?"

He heard his name and turned to see his mum in the car park. Abdullah's heart sank as he walked slowly towards his mum and thought,

"Dad is always working..."

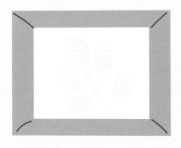

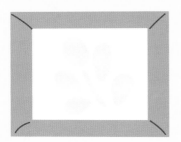

Abdullah and his mum sat down to have dinner.
He told his mum all about saying JazakAllah Khair and
the homework that his mualimah had given him to do.

"I think I'll make a JazakAllah Khair card for you Mum,"
Abdullah said. "You woke me up in the morning, and
made me delicious pancakes and even picked me up
from Arabic class. You deserve all my gratitude."

Abdullah's mum smiled and hugged him.

"But what about your Dad?" she asked, "can you think
of anything that he did for you this morning?"

Abdullah shrugged his shoulders and said,

"Dad is always working..."

"Hmmm that's true," responded Mum, "but this morning did you notice that your clothes were already laid out nice and neatly, your bike was fixed and even your football boots were super clean?"

Abdullah's mind raced back to breakfast time when he saw his dad with muddy marks on his shirt before he rushed out of the door.

"Did Dad do **ALL** of that?" Abdullah whispered. Abdullah's mum nodded.

"For me?" Abdullah's mum smiled and nodded once more.

"There are a lot of things that you may not see that your father does for you, because he loves you," said Mum.

Abdullah realised that his dad must have been late because he had spent his morning ironing, fixing and even cleaning!

He ran to his room, got out his colouring pens and got to work, to make his dad the most amazing JazakAllah Khair card ever.

As he worked, he thought about how his dad has to work hard to make sure that he and his mum could live in their beautiful house and eat all the tasty food in the kitchen.

JazakAllah Khair
DAD

Once he had finished, Abdullah tiptoed into his dad's room and placed the card in his jacket pocket.

The next morning, Abdullah's dad was sitting at his desk, typing away frantically at his computer. He felt a piece of card in his pocket and pulled it out.

It was covered in his favourite teal colour with a picture of a little boy, a bike, a pair of football boots and the biggest stack of pancakes ever.

"JazakAllah Khair - May Allah Reward You with Goodness (AND lots of pancakes), for all the things that you do for me, that I see and that I do not see.

I am very thankful, and I know that even when you're working, it is because you love me!"

From your son,

Abdullah

22

Abdullah and his mum arrived home in the evening after football, as soon as they opened the front door, they smelt something burning coming from the kitchen.

They ran into the kitchen to see what on earth was going on. Abdullah's dad was standing in the middle of the kitchen sweating, covered in flour and holding a stack of very burnt pancakes.

"Dad … are … you … okay?" said Abdullah as he and his mum struggled to hold back their laughter.

"Dinner is served!" Abdullah's dad announced importantly as he wiped some flour off of his face.

After a rather crunchy meal, as they all began cleaning up the kitchen, Abdullah thought to himself,

"Dad is always working...

...for ME!"

24